· THE ·
PATCHWORK QUILT

VALERIE FLOURNOY AND JERRY PINKNEY

PUFFIN BOOKS

D0315939

PUFFIN BOOKS

Published by the Penguin Group
Penguin Books Ltd, 27 Wrights Lane, London W8 5TZ, England
Penguin Books USA Inc., 375 Hudson Street, New York, New York 10014, USA
Penguin Books Australia Ltd, Ringwood, Victoria, Australia
Penguin Books Canada Ltd, 10 Alcorn Avenue, Toronto, Ontario, Canada M4V 3B2
Penguin Books (NZ) Ltd, 182–190 Wairau Road, Auckland 10, New Zealand

Penguin Books Ltd, Registered Offices: Harmondsworth, Middlesex, England

First published by The Bodley Head 1985
First published in Picture Puffin 1987
Reissued in Puffin Books 1995
1 3 5 7 9 10 8 6 4 2

Text copyright © Valerie Flournoy, 1985
Illustrations copyright © Jerry Pinkney, 1985
All rights reserved

Made and printed in Italy by Printers srl – Trento

To my grandmother Rose Buchanan
and my mother, Ivie Mae Flournoy

V.F.

To Gloria and my father

J.P.

Tanya sat restlessly on her chair by the kitchen window. For several days she had had a cold and had had to stay in bed. But the cold was almost gone now, and Tanya was anxious to go outside and enjoy the fresh air and the arrival of spring.

"Mama, when can I go outside?" she asked.

Mama pulled a tray of biscuits from the oven and placed it on the worktop. "In time," she murmured. "All in good time."

Tanya gazed through the window and saw Papa and her two brothers, Ted and Jim, building the new garden fence.

"I'm going to talk to Grandma," she said.

Grandma was sitting in her favourite spot – the big soft chair in front of the picture window. In her lap were scraps of material of all textures and colours. Tanya recognized some of them. The check was from Papa's old work shirt, and the red scraps were from the shirt Ted had worn that winter.

"What are you going to do with all that stuff?" Tanya asked.

"*Stuff?* These ain't stuff. These little pieces gonna make me a quilt, a patchwork quilt."

Tanya tilted her head. "I know what a quilt is, Grandma. There's one on your bed, but it's old and dirty and Mama can never get it clean."

Grandma sighed. "It ain't dirty, honey. It's worn, the way it's supposed to be."

Grandma flexed her fingers to keep them from stiffening. She sucked in some air and said, "My mother made me that quilt when I wasn't any older than you. But sometimes the old ways are forgotten."

Tanya leaned against the chair and rested her head on her grandmother's shoulder.

Just then Mama walked in with two glasses of milk and some biscuits. She looked at the scraps of material that were scattered everywhere. "Grandma," she said, "I've just tidied this room, and now it's a mess."

"It's not a mess, Mama," Tanya said, through a mouthful of biscuit. "It's a quilt."

"A quilt! You don't need these scraps. I can get you a quilt," Mama said.

Grandma looked at her daughter and then turned to her grandchild. "Yes, your mama can get you a quilt from any department store. But it won't be like my patchwork quilt, and it won't last as long either."

Mama looked at Grandma, then picked up Tanya's empty glass and went to make lunch.

Grandma's eyes grew dark and distant. She turned away from Tanya and gazed out of the window, absentmindedly rubbing the pieces of material through her fingers.

"Grandma, I'll help you make your quilt," Tanya said.

"Thank you, honey."

"Let's start right now. We'll be finished in no time."

Grandma held Tanya close and patted her head. "It's gonna take quite a while to make this quilt, not a couple of days or a week – not even a month. A good quilt, a masterpiece. . ." Grandma's eyes shone at the thought. "Why, I need more material. More gold and blue, some red and green. And I'll need the time to do it right. It'll take me a year at least."

"A year!" shouted Tanya. "That's too long. I can't wait that long, Grandma."

Grandma laughed. "A year ain't that long, honey. Makin' this quilt gonna be a joy. Now run along and let Grandma rest." Grandma turned her head towards the sunlight and closed her eyes.

"I'm gonna make a masterpiece," she murmured, clutching a scrap of cloth in her hand, just before she fell asleep.

"We'll have to get you a new pair of jeans and use these old ones for rags," Mama said as she hung Jim's blue corduroy trousers on the clothesline one August afternoon.

Jim was miserable. The corduroy jeans had been his favourite and now they were beyond repair.

"Bring them here," Grandma said.

She took the jeans and cut a few blue squares from one of the legs. Jim gave her a hug, as he watched her add his patches to the others.

"A quilt won't forget. It can tell your life story," she said.

Autumn came and Mama made Tanya an African princess costume for a fancy dress party. The old bracelets and earrings Tanya had found in a trunk in the attic jingled noisily as she danced round in the long, flowing robes Mama had made from several yards of colourful material. Grandma cut some squares out of the leftover scraps and added Tanya to the quilt too!

The days grew colder, but Tanya and her brothers didn't mind. They knew snow wasn't far away. Mama dreaded winter's coming. Every year she would plead with Grandma to move away from the draughty window, but Grandma wouldn't budge.

"Grandma, please," Mama scolded. "You can sit here by the heater."

"I'm not your grandmother, I'm your mother," Grandma said. "And I'm gonna sit here in the Lord's light and make my masterpiece."

One morning at the end of November Tanya woke up to find everything in sight covered with snow. She got dressed and rushed downstairs. Ted and Jim, and even Mama and Papa, were already outside.

"I don't like leaving Grandma in that house by herself," Mama said. "I know she's lonely."

"Grandma isn't lonely," Tanya said. "She and the quilt are telling each other stories."

Mama glanced curiously at Tanya, "Telling each other stories?"

"Yes, Grandma says a quilt never forgets!"

The family spent the morning and most of the afternoon tobogganing down the hill. Finally, when they were all numb from the cold, they went inside for something warm to eat.

"I think I'll go and sit with Grandma," Mama said.

"Then she can explain to you about our quilt – our very own family quilt," Tanya said.

Mama saw the mischievous glint in Tanya's eyes.

"Why, I may just have her to do that, young lady," she said, as she walked out of the kitchen.

Tanya leaned over the table to look into the living-room. Grandma was hunched over, her eyes close to the fabric as she made tiny stitches. Mama sat at the old woman's feet. Tanya couldn't hear what was said, but she knew Grandma was telling Mama all about quilts and how *this* quilt would be very special. Tanya sipped her chocolate slowly, then she saw Mama pick up a piece of fabric, rub it with her fingers and smile.

From that moment on both women spent their winter evenings working on the quilt. Mama did the sewing while Grandma cut the material and placed the scraps in a pattern of colours. Even while they were cooking and baking all their specialities for Christmas during the day, they still worked on the quilt at night. Only once did Mama put it aside. She wanted to wear something special for Christmas, so she bought some gold material and made a beautiful dress. Tanya knew without asking that the gold scraps would be in the quilt too.

There was much singing and laughing that Christmas. All Grandma's sons and daughters and nieces and nephews came over for the day. The Christmas tree lights shone brightly, filling the room with sparkling colours. Later, when everyone had gone home, Papa said he had never felt so much happiness in the house. And Mama agreed.

When Tanya got downstairs the next morning, she found Papa and the boys alone in the kitchen.

"Where's Mama?" she asked.

"Grandma doesn't feel well this morning," Papa said. "Your mother is with her now till the doctor gets here."

"Will Grandma be all right?" Ted asked.

Papa rubbed his son's head and smiled. "There's nothing for you to worry about. We'll take care of Grandma."

Tanya looked into the living-room. There on the back of the big chair rested the patchwork quilt. It was folded neatly, just as Grandma had left it.

"Mother didn't want us to know she wasn't feeling well. She thought it would spoil our Christmas," Mama told them later. She looked drawn and tired, and her eyes were a puffy red. "Now it's up to all of us to be quiet and make her as comfortable as possible." Papa put an arm around Mama's shoulder.

"Can we see Grandma?" Tanya asked.

"No, not tonight," Papa said. "Grandma needs plenty of rest."

It wasn't until New Year's Eve that the children were allowed to see their grandmother. She looked tired and spoke in whispers.

"We miss you, Grandma," Ted said.

"And your gingerbread and hot chocolate," added Jim. Grandma smiled.

"Your quilt misses you too, Grandma," Tanya said. Grandma's smile faded from her lips. Her eyes grew cloudy.

"My masterpiece," Grandma sighed. "It would have been beautiful. Almost half finished." She closed her eyes and turned away. Papa whispered it was time to leave, and Ted, Jim and Tanya crept out of the room.

Tanya walked slowly over to where the quilt lay. She had seen Grandma and Mama work on it. Tanya thought about it for a moment. She knew how to cut the scraps, but she wasn't certain of the rest. Just then Tanya felt a hand resting on her shoulder. She looked up and saw Mama.

"Tomorrow," Mama said.

New Year's Day was the beginning. After the dishes had been washed up and put away, Tanya and Mama examined the quilt.

"You cut more squares, Tanya, while I stitch some patches together," Mama said.

Tanya snipped and trimmed the scraps of material till her hands hurt from the scissors. Mama watched her carefully, making sure the squares were all the same size. The next day was the same as the last. More snipping and cutting. But Mama couldn't always be around to watch Tanya work. Grandma had to be looked after. So Tanya worked by herself. Then one night, when Papa was reading them stories, Jim walked over and looked at the quilt. In it he saw patches of blue. His blue. Without saying a word Jim picked up the scissors and some scraps and started to make squares. Ted helped Jim put the squares in piles while Mama showed Tanya how to join them together.

Every day, as soon as she got home from school, Tanya worked on the quilt. Ted and Jim were too busy playing sport, and Mama was looking after Grandma, so Tanya worked alone. But after a few weeks she stopped. Something was wrong – something was missing, Tanya thought. For days the quilt lay on the back of the chair. No one knew why Tanya had stopped working. Tanya would just sit and look at the quilt. Suddenly she knew what was wrong. Some*thing* wasn't missing. Some*one* was missing from the quilt.

That evening before she went to bed Tanya tiptoed into Grandma's room. She quietly lifted the end of Grandma's old quilt and carefully cut out a few squares.

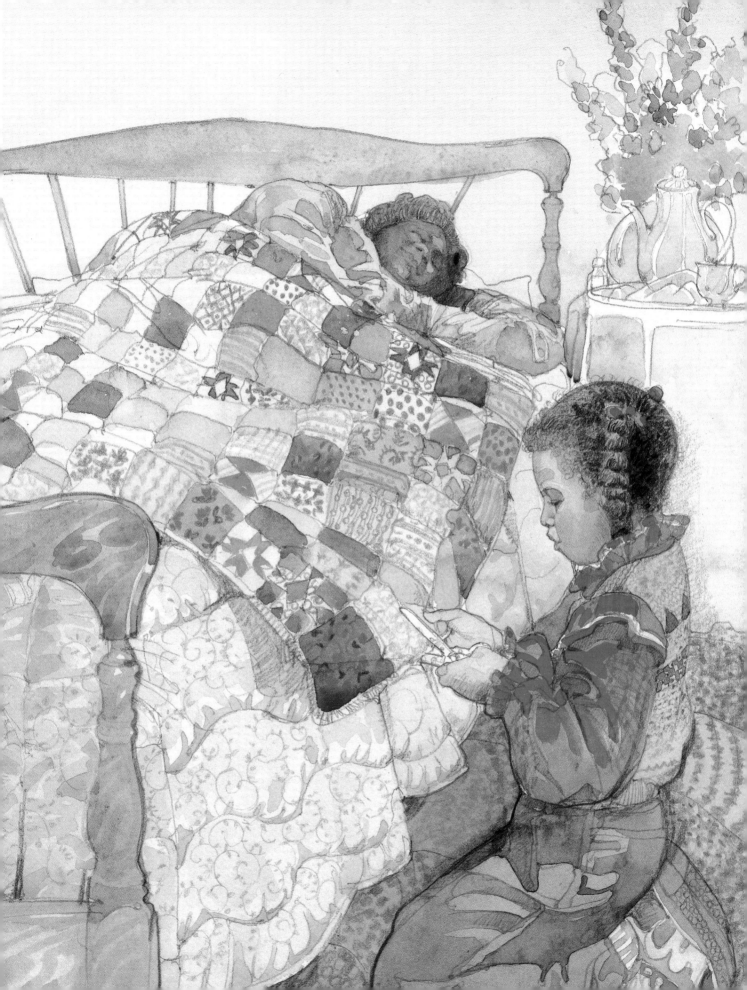

February and March came and went as Mama proudly watched her daughter work on the last few rows of patches. Tanya always found time for the quilt.

Grandma had been watching too. She had been getting stronger and stronger as the months passed. Once she was well enough, Papa would carry her to her chair by the window. "I needs the Lord's light," Grandma would say. Then she would sit and hum softly to herself and watch Tanya work.

"Yes, honey, this quilt is nothin' but a joy," Grandma said.

Summer was almost here. One June day Tanya came home to find Grandma working on the quilt again! She had finished sewing the last few squares together, the stuffing was in place and she was already pinning on the backing.

"Grandma!" Tanya shouted.

Grandma looked up. "Hush, child. It's almost time to do the quilting on these patches. But first I have some special finishing touches. . ."

The next night Grandma cut the final thread with her teeth. "There. It's done," she said. Mama helped Grandma spread the quilt full length.

Nobody realized how big the quilt had grown, or how beautiful it was. Reds, greens, blues and golds, light colours and dark, blended in and out throughout the quilt.

"It's beautiful," Papa said. He touched the gold patch, looked at Mama and remembered. Jim remembered too – there was his blue and the red from Ted's shirt. There was Tanya's African princess costume. And there was Grandma. And even though her patch was old, it fitted perfectly with the rest.

They all remembered the past year. They especially remembered Tanya and all her hard work, and there, in the righthand
corner of the last row of patches, was delicately stitched, "For
Tanya from your Mama and Grandma".

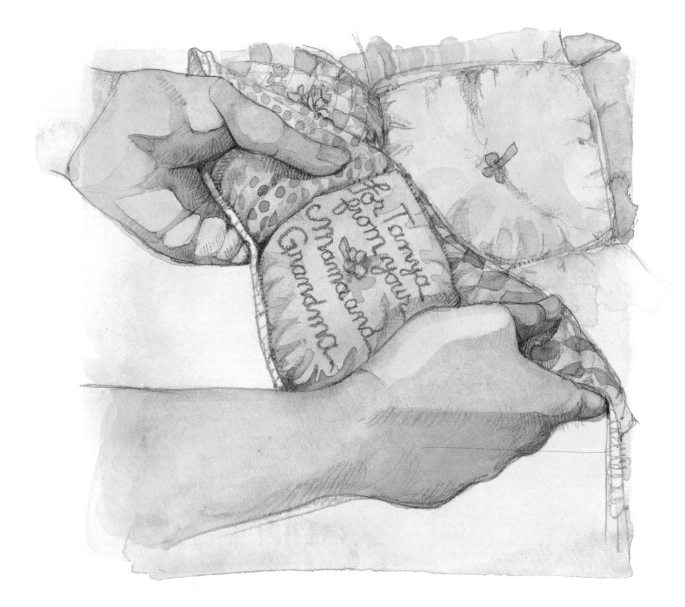